HERCULES

THE COMPLETE MYTHS
OF A LEGENDARY HERO

WITH AN AFTERWORD
BY GEORGES MOROZ

Published by
Bantam Doubleday Dell Books for Young Readers
a division of
Bantam Doubleday Dell Publishing Group, Inc.
1540 Broadway
New York, New York 10036

Map by Heather Saunders
Interior art by Chris Spollen
Book design by Julie E. Baker

The trademark Laurel-Leaf Library® is registered in the U.S. Patent and Trademark Office.
The trademark Dell® is registered in the U.S. Patent and Trademark Office.

ISBN: 0-440-22732-1
Printed in the United States of America
June 1997
10 9 8 7 6 5 4 3 2 1

There is a saying among men, put forth long ago, that you cannot rightly judge whether a mortal's lot is good or evil before he dies.

Sophocles, *The Women of Trachis*

GODS OF MOUNT OLYMPUS

(a partial list)

GREEK NAME OF GOD *(Roman name of god)*

APHRODITE *(Venus)*
    goddess of love

APOLLO *(Helios)*
    god of the sun

ARES *(Mars)*
    god of war

ARTEMIS *(Diana)*
    goddess of the moon and of the hunt

ATHENA *(Minerva)*
    goddess of wisdom and battle

DEMETER *(Ceres)*
    goddess of the harvest

DIONYSUS *(Bacchus)*
    god of wine

HEPHAESTUS *(Vulcan)*
    god of fire

HERA *(Juno)*
    queen of Mount Olympus/goddess of marriage

HERMES *(Mercury)*
    messenger of the gods

POSEIDON *(Neptune)*
    god of the sea

ZEUS *(Jupiter)*
    king of Mount Olympus/god of thunder

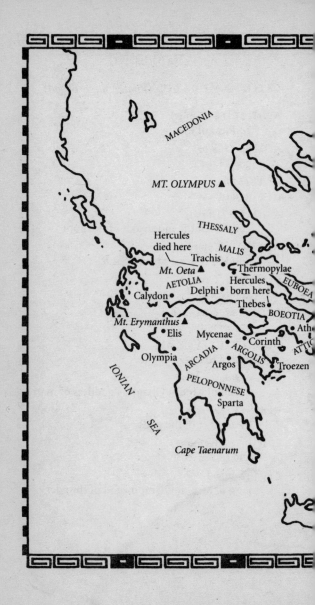

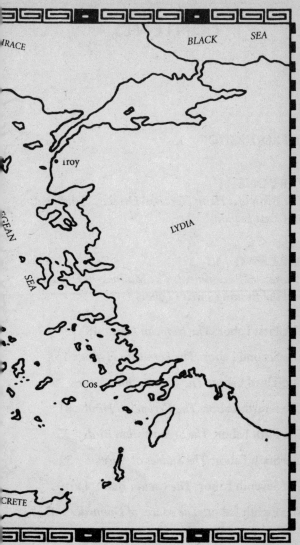

THRACE

BLACK   SEA

Troy

LYDIA

AEGEAN

SEA

Cos

CRETE

CONTENTS

INTRODUCTION

Hercules,* the most illustrious figure in all of Greek mythology, is also the most popular hero-god among readers of classical literature. His name immediately conjures up raw strength—strength Hercules used in battling all sorts of monstrous creatures in order to complete the famous twelve labors imposed on him. Few readers, however, know that Hercules submitted to these labors because of his lifelong nemesis, Hera, the queen of the gods on Mount Olympus.

As Zeus' wife, Hera was jealous because her husband had fathered a child with a mortal woman. Hercules was this child. From his birth, Hera set out to destroy him, and though she never succeeded, she was respon-

---

Hercules is the Roman name for *Heracles*. This book uses *Hercules* as the more common form. All other names are Greek.

sible for much of his life's agony. Hera used her godly powers to drive Hercules mad; in his delusional state, Hercules slaughtered all three of his children from his first marriage. His punishment: the twelve labors. Successfully completing the labors was Hercules' only way to expiate the sin of his hideous crime and to achieve purification and eventual immortality. This theme of crime, punishment, and atonement is one that Hercules repeats several times before dying and ascending to his status of Greek god.

It is ironic that Hercules' very name—in the Greek appellation Heracles—means "Hera's Glory," and that the twelve labors he carried out ultimately resulted in her glorification. But Hercules' trials and triumphs, and Hera's involvement in them, were all prophesied by the Oracle at Delphi. And so it can be said that the gods do work in mysterious ways.

PART ONE

———

THE BIRTH OF A HERO: HERCULES' ORIGINS, CHILDHOOD, AND FIRST EXPLOITS

Hercules, son of Zeus and Alcmene and the stepson of Amphitryon, king of Troezen, was born into a distinguished lineage. Not only was his father the ruler of the gods on Mount Olympus, but his mother and stepfather's grandfather was Perseus, who slew Medusa, one of the three female monsters known as Gorgons whose head was so fearful that anyone who had the misfortune of looking at it turned to stone. Perseus was also the son of Zeus; his mother was Danaë. The region of Argos in the Peloponnese fell under his and his descendants' control.

Electryon, son of Perseus and father to Alcmene and her eight brothers, was king of Mycenae, a city in the northeast corner of the plain of Argos. His cattle had been stolen by the Teleboans, who killed his eight sons during the raid. Seeking revenge, Electryon pursued his enemies, while his nephew Amphitryon, king of the neighboring city of Troezen, acted as regent; Alcmene, Electryon's daughter, had been betrothed to him.

Hearing that the king of Elis had seized the stolen cattle and was asking for a hefty ransom, Amphitryon agreed to pay and recalled Electryon to identify the animals. The king of Mycenae, furious at being asked to repay Amphitryon for the ransom, accused him of condoning a fraud. Enraged by the accusation, Amphitryon vented his anger by throwing a club at a stray cow; but the club rebounded from the cow's horns and killed Electryon. Subsequently Amphitryon's uncle Sthenelus used the mishap to banish his nephew from the whole of Argos and to seize the throne of Mycenae.

Amphitryon fled to Thebes, the main city of Boeotia, with Alcmene and was purified by King Creon. But though Alcmene, whose name meant "strong in wrath," married Amphitryon, she refused to consummate the

4

marriage until he had avenged her eight brothers' deaths. So Amphitryon undertook an expedition against the Teleboans with the help of Creon and soundly defeated them.

During Amphitryon's absence, Zeus, who longed for beautiful Alcmene, deceived her by assuming the body of her husband. He further misled Alcmene by giving her a gold cup that had belonged to Pterelas, king of the Teleboans, and told her of the exploits accomplished by Amphitryon during the expedition, ascribing them to himself and assuring her that her brothers were avenged. Wholly deceived, Alcmene listened with delight to the god's account of the defeat inflicted on Pterelas.

A long night of love between the disguised Zeus and Alcmene ensued—a night that was prolonged at Zeus' command so as to have the length of three. On this night, Hercules was conceived. When a victorious Amphitryon returned to Thebes on the following day, he was surprised by his wife's lack of enthusiasm in welcoming him home. He was equally surprised by what she said: "After a sleepless night, I hope you do not expect me to hear a second time the story of your military feats!" Still, Alcmene returned her husband's amorous advances and Amphitryon gave her a second son, Iphicles, Hercules' twin brother, younger by one night. But puzzled by his wife's remarks, Amphitryon consulted the seer Tiresias, who told him that he had been cuckolded by Zeus.

Hera, Zeus' wife, was aware of her husband's infidelity (it wasn't the first time his eyes had wandered) and the fact that he had fathered a son with Alcmene. Her jealousy and wrath were extreme. She wanted revenge, and knowing that Zeus had decreed that the first child born into the race of the Perseides would one day rule over Argos, Hera enlisted the help of her daughter Eileithyia, the goddess of childbirth. Together they conspired to delay Hercules' birth, while speeding up that of his cousin Eurystheus, the son of Sthenelus. And so Eurystheus was born at seven months, Hercules and his twin, Iphicles, at ten months.

Upon Hercules' birth, Alcmene, who had been warned by Athena of Hera's jealousy, took her newborn to a field outside Thebes, where he lay until Athena, following Zeus' suggestion, took Hera there for a stroll. Athena stopped next to the infant and pretended to be impressed by the baby's vigor and beauty. She asked Hera to give him her breast, which Hera did. But Hercules sucked with such force and lust that the goddess flung him away in pain. A jet of milk is said to have flown across the sky and formed the trail of stars known as the Milky Way. Athena picked the baby up and returned him to Alcmene, instructing her to raise him without fear. Baby Hercules, having sucked at the breast of Hera, his cruelest enemy, had fulfilled a requisite to achieve immortality.

Hera's fury did not abate. One evening, when Hercules was ten months old, Hera sent two enormous snakes into the room where he and Iphicles were sleeping. The snakes slithered into the spacious chamber, eager to clamp their deadly jaws around the innocent babies. Iphicles started to cry, but Hercules was far from helpless and frightened. He simply strangled the two snakes with his bare hands. This was Hercules' first taste of battle.

Amphitryon, who had seized his sword and rushed into the nursery upon hearing Iphicles' cries, was stunned by what he witnessed. Later that morning, he went to see Tiresias again and told him of Hercules' extraordinary feat; the seer then foretold Hercules' glories to come. But some claim that Amphitryon placed the snakes in the cradle because he was intensely curious to know which of the twins was his son. And now he knew for sure.

Hercules' strength increased with age, as did his skills. Amphitryon taught him how to drive a chariot; Eurytus, grandson of the god Apollo, showed him how to use the bow; and Castor, brother of Helen of Troy, instructed him in the handling of arms. Most of his lessons, however, came from Linus, a musician who tutored him in literature and music. But Hercules was headstrong and given to unruly behavior. All too frequently pupil and tutor clashed. One day, during a lyre lesson, Linus tried to beat his stubborn student; but Hercules lost his temper, seized the lyre, and dealt his master such a blow that Linus died instantly. Tried for murder, Hercules quoted a law that justified killing an aggressor in self-defense and thus was acquitted. But Amphitryon, fearing the recurrence of such fits of murderous rage, sent Hercules off to the country and put him in charge of his herds of cattle. Hercules remained there until his eighteenth year, growing in strength as well as in size to reach a height of seven feet.

Now a young man, Hercules left the cattle ranch and carried out his first exploit by killing the lion of Cithaeron. This wild beast, outstanding in its size and ferociousness, caused considerable havoc among the herds of Amphitryon and of Thespius, who ruled over a city near Thebes. Hercules set out to destroy the lion. He moved into Thespius' domain, spent his days out hunting, and returned to the palace at night to sleep. After fifty days, he finally tracked down the lion and smashed its head with a club cut from an olive tree.

King Thespius was grateful as well as eager to have his grandchildren fathered by Hercules. He offered his eldest daughter as Hercules' paramour. But King Thespius had a total of fifty daughters by his wife Megamede, and on each subsequent night, another of the daughters visited Hercules in the darkness, until he had lain with them all. All along, Hercules believed that he was sleeping with the same woman. The daughters of Thespius bore him fifty sons, who were known as the Thespiades. But some say that, showing for the first time his stunning sexual appetite, Hercules enjoyed the fifty daughters in a single night.

Upon his journey back to Thebes, Hercules crossed paths with the envoys of Erginus, king of Orchomenus in Boeotia. They were on their way to Thebes to collect a yearly tribute. Years before, Clymenus, the local king, had been mortally wounded by a Theban charioteer at a festival in honor of the god Poseidon. Carried dying to Orchomenus, Clymenus charged his son Erginus to avenge his death. So Erginus marched against the Thebans, soundly defeated them, and concluded with them a treaty by which they would pay him an annual tribute of one hundred cattle for twenty years. So when Hercules inquired about their business, the envoys replied that they were about to remind the Thebans of Erginus' generosity in not cutting off the ears, nose, and hands of every citizen. Enraged by their arrogance, Hercules mutilated the heralds according to their description and fastened their bloody extremities by ropes from their necks. He then told them to carry that tribute back to their master. Indignant at this outrage, Erginus marched against Thebes. Hercules armed the Thebans and led the charge. He ambushed his enemies in a narrow pass and killed Erginus. Thereafter he took over and sacked Orchomenus, which was compelled to pay double the tribute to Thebes. Tragically, Amphitryon lost his life during the campaign while fighting bravely alongside his stepson.

King Creon gave Hercules his eldest daughter, Megara, in marriage, a fitting prize for his having saved the city. By her, Hercules had three sons: Therimachus, Creontiades, and Deicoon. And Creon gave his younger daughter to Iphicles.

PART TWO

CRIME AND PUNISHMENT: THE MADNESS OF HERCULES AND THE ENSUING TWELVE LABORS

Hera's wrath toward Hercules did not decrease with time. On the contrary, the mounting glory of the young hero was for her a constant reminder of the humiliating deception she had had to endure. But Hercules' refusal to acknowledge his cousin Eurystheus as the firstborn among Perseus' great-grandchildren—and therefore as the ruler of Argolis (the area encompassing Argos and Mycenae)—went against Zeus' edict. This played right into Hera's desire for vengeance, and she felt justified in submitting Hercules to divine retribution.

The queen of the gods tricked Hercules into believing that his three children by Megara were his deadliest enemies. And so Hercules murdered them. The crimes took place in front of the Temple of Zeus, where the sons and their mother were about to attend a sacrifice. Hercules approached them like a madman, his eyes bulging and his veins engorged. Then he laughed a sinister laugh and aimed his bow at his sons. The children rushed away in terror. The first tried to hide behind a pillar, but Hercules chased him in circles and finally pierced his heart with an arrow. The second child fell at his father's knees and cried, "Dearest Father, do not murder me!" Unmoved, Hercules seized his club and smashed his son's skull. The third son rushed toward his mother, who pulled him into the temple and locked the doors. In his murderous rage, Hercules pried open the doors and ruthlessly plunged his sword into the boy's chest.

When Hercules returned to his senses, he was overwhelmed by grief and, thinking of suicide, cried out, "Why spare the life of the man who killed my sons? To avenge the murder of my children, let me hurl myself from a cliff, or expel with fire the madness that seized my body!" But all Hercules could do was flee from human contact, so ridden was he with despair, shame, and puzzlement over his crimes. In

16

exile he sought advice from Apollo's Oracle in Delphi on how he might be purified. The Pythoness told him to go to Mycenae in the western part of Argolis and to serve Eurystheus, who reigned over that city. His servitude was to last twelve years. The Pythoness also advised him to perform whatever labors his cousin might impose upon him, for he would be rewarded with immortality.

Hercules found it repugnant to serve a man who was so far from being his equal and who was known for his cowardice and mediocrity. But determined to atone for his hideous crimes as well as to comply with the gods' incomprehensible demands, Hercules accepted the enslavement to Eurystheus and the ensuing trials.

Hercules set forth on his labors, having received many gifts: Athena gave him a golden breastplate, Hephaestus a helmet, Apollo a bow, Hermes a sword; from Poseidon he received his horses, and from Zeus a splendid shield decorated with enamel and gold. But Hercules' most distinctive weapon was to be the club he had fashioned while hunting the lion of Cithaeron.

THE FIRST LABOR

THE NEMEAN LION

The first labor imposed on Hercules was the slaying of the Nemean lion, a gigantic beast with a pelt impervious to both iron and stone. The monster, whose sibling was the famous and deadly Sphinx of Thebes, had been brought up by Hera and released in the region of Nemea in Argolis. There, it had been devouring people and herds with unrestrained ferocity. Hercules surprised the lion as it was about to enter its cave. The beast was covered with blood from the day's slaughter. He shot several arrows at it, but this was in vain, as they rebounded from the pelt without inflicting any injury. An assault with the sword was similarly fruitless. Finally Hercules, using his club, dealt the monster a violent blow on the muzzle, driving the

21

somewhat shaken lion into its cave. Not wasting a second, he blocked one of the two exits with heavy rocks and entered by the other. Having realized that weapons were futile against such a formidable adversary, Hercules decided to wrestle the creature. He wrapped his arms around the lion's neck, slowly choking the monster, which died in the midst of savage convulsions. When he tried to flay the lion, Hercules was at a loss as to how to pierce the impenetrable skin. He finally thought of using the beast's own razor-sharp claws to cut it, and proudly wore the invulnerable pelt as armor.

Thus clad in the lion skin, with the beast's gigantic corpse slung across his shoulders, Hercules returned to Thebes. His appearance terrified Eurystheus, who ordered him to leave the fruits of his labors outside the gates in the future. Some claim that Zeus added the lion to the constellations to celebrate his son's exploit.

THE SECOND LABOR

THE LERNAEAN HYDRA

As a second labor, Eurystheus ordered the destruction of another monster reared by Hera, the Lernaean Hydra. It had a doglike body and seven snakelike heads, one of them immortal. The breath coming from its mouths was so venomous that it meant a sure death for anyone approaching it. The Hydra was living near Argos by a grove of plane trees stretching down to the sea. It had its lair in a swamp surrounding the source of the river Amymone and was ravaging the countryside, destroying the crops, and terrorizing people and animals. The goddess Athena helped Hercules find the Hydra's lair and advised him to attack the monster with burning arrows so as to force it out of its refuge. But each time Hercules crushed one of the Hydra's heads with his club, it grew back instantly. The help of his nephew Iolaus, son of Iphicles, was crucial at this point. At Hercules' request, Iolaus set the grove on fire and supplied Hercules with burning brands, with which he was able to sear each headless neck. And with a sword, Hercules severed the central head, which was immortal, and buried it under a huge rock. Then he dipped his arrows in the Hydra's blood, making each one so poisonous that the smallest wound inflicted by it would be fatal.

THE THIRD LABOR

THE ERYMANTHIAN BOAR

The third labor imposed on Hercules was to bring back alive a monstrous boar that haunted the cypress-covered slopes of Mount Erymanthus in Arcadia. The fierce and enormous beast was dislodged from a thicket by Hercules' fearsome shouts and then driven into the deep snow that covered the mountain. Chasing the boar until exhaustion, Hercules eventually jumped on its back, bound it with chains, and brought it to Mycenae on his shoulders. When Eurystheus saw it, he was once more struck with terror and hid in a big bronze jar he had secretly prepared as a refuge in time of danger.

THE FOURTH LABOR

THE CERYNEIAN HIND

As a fourth labor, Hercules was to capture the hind of Ceryneia and bring it alive to Mycenae. This very large creature was one of five hinds that Artemis, a child at that time, had once seen grazing on Mount Lycaeus in Thessaly. They all had golden horns and were larger than bulls. The goddess, running in pursuit, caught four of them and harnessed them to her chariot. The fifth fled to the Ceryneian Hill, guided by Hera, who already had Hercules' labors in mind. As the hind was sacred to Artemis, it was considered an act of impiety to kill or even to touch it. Hercules intended to perform his labor without exerting the least force.

He hunted the swift animal for a year, going as far north as the land of the Hyperboreans;

there, he visited the fabled people who worship Apollo. Weary from the chase, the beast took refuge on Mount Artemisium, where Hercules pinned its forelegs with an arrow and caught it. He put it on his shoulders and hastened through Arcadia to Mycenae. But Artemis and Apollo blocked his path, intent on depriving him of the hind, which they considered their property. Hercules pleaded with them, laying the blame on Eurystheus. This appeased the anger of Artemis and her brother, and Hercules was allowed to carry the beast alive to Mycenae.

THE FIFTH LABOR

THE STYMPHALIAN BIRDS

The fifth labor Eurystheus imposed on Hercules was to chase away man-eating birds living on the shores of Lake Stymphalus in Arcadia. They had multiplied to the point of becoming a plague to the surroundings, ravaging the crops with their poisonous excrement. In addition, they were taking to the air in great flocks, attacking men and beasts with their brazen beaks and claws, which could pierce a metal breastplate. They also poured showers of their brazen feathers down like arrows.

After having tried without success to drive them away with his bow and arrows, Hercules received the help of Athena, who gave him castanets of bronze made by Hephaestus. Standing on a mountain, overlooking the lake, Hercules clacked the castanets and created such a din that the terrified birds assembled in a gigantic flock and flew away, going as far as the Black Sea. Immediately Hercules shot at the dense pack with his arrows and slaughtered many of the birds.

THE SIXTH LABOR

THE STABLES OF AUGEIAS

Hercules' sixth labor was to be the cleansing of Augeias' filthy cattle yard in one day. Augeias, son of the sun, Helios, was king of Elis, a city located near Olympia in the Peloponnese. Helios had given him huge herds of cattle, so that Augeias was the wealthiest man in Greece. But through deplorable neglect, the dung in the cattle yard had not been cleared away for years and lay in a thick layer through which it was no longer possible to plow for grain—resulting in a stench that affected the entire Peloponnese.

Eurystheus could not disguise his glee at the idea of sending Hercules to that pestilent and sterile land, and he pictured with malice his cousin's humiliation at having to load the dung into baskets and carry them on his shoulders.

Before starting work, Hercules struck a deal with Augeias: The king would give him a tenth of his herds if Hercules succeeded in cleaning the stables within the one day commanded by Eurystheus. Hercules did not waste a minute and, after having pierced a breach in the foundations of the cattle yard, undertook to divert the flow of two neighboring rivers, the Alpheius and the Peneius. As a result, the two rivers rushed through the yard and swept it clean. Subsequently the vigorous flow went on to cleanse the pastures, and by nightfall the land was restored to health. But Augeias did not keep his word and refused to pay the reward that they had agreed upon, claiming that the river gods had done the job.

THE SEVENTH LABOR

THE CRETAN BULL

Hercules was ordered to capture the Cretan bull as his seventh labor. The beast had been the lover of Pasiphaë, daughter of the Sun (Helios) and wife of Minos, the king of Crete. As Minos, breaking an earlier promise, had refused to sacrifice to Poseidon a fine bull, the god of the sea punished him by inspiring in Pasiphaë a passion for the bull. The Minotaur, a monster who had the body of a man and the head of a bull, was the result of their union. Hercules went to Crete and met Minos, who allowed him to capture the bull. He caught the beautiful and ferocious beast without assistance after a long struggle and brought it back to Greece. Eurystheus wanted to dedicate the bull to Hera, but the goddess refused to accept an offering so closely associated with Hercules' glory. She set it free and the beast wandered through Argos and the Isthmus of Corinth to Attica, where it was captured by Theseus, king of Athens, and sacrificed to Athena.

THE EIGHTH LABOR

THE MARES OF DIOMEDES

Diomedes was a king of the Bistones, a warlike Thracian people. His stables, in which four savage mares lived, were the terror of Thrace. The untamable mares were fed on the flesh of unsuspecting guests and were so ferocious that they were permanently tethered with iron chains. Eurystheus ordered Hercules to capture them and bring them back alive.

Accompanied by a small troop of volunteers, Hercules set sail and landed on the coast of Thrace. Upon finding the stables, Hercules and his men massacred the grooms and captured Diomedes. Hercules set the king before his own mares, which tore his body apart and devoured him. Calmer after having satisfied their appetite for human flesh and kept solidly bound to each other, the four mares were led to the ship and brought to Mycenae.

THE NINTH LABOR

THE GIRDLE OF
QUEEN HIPPOLYTE

At the order of Eurystheus' daughter Admete, Hercules was to capture the golden girdle given by Ares to Hippolyte, queen of the Amazons. A nation of female warriors stemming from Ares, the Amazons had excluded men from their society except for reproduction, intermittently associating with men from neighboring tribes for this purpose. All their infant boys were put to death or had their arms and legs broken so that they were incapacitated. Girls, on the other hand, were reared in a manly fashion, handling weapons and riding horses. The Amazons clad themselves in the skins of wild beasts and cut off their right breasts to facilitate the use of weapons in battle. Hunting and fighting on horseback were their main occupations, and so savage and unrestrained was their behavior that they terrified even the most seasoned warriors.

Hercules set sail in one ship with a number of volunteers. After having passed the Bosphorus and sailed through the Black Sea, they arrived at Themiscyra, the harbor of the Amazons' country. Hippolyte visited Hercules, and, both intrigued by his fame and attracted by his muscular body, she promised to give him the girdle. But Hera, disguised in the likeness of an Amazon, started spreading a rumor that the strangers who had arrived were planning to abduct the queen. So armed Amazons charged the ship on horseback.

When Hercules saw them, he suspected treachery, killed Hippolyte, and stripped her of the girdle. He and his troops then proceeded to put the Amazonian army to flight after great slaughter. But some claim that Hippolyte refused to give up the girdle and that battle ensued; and that Hercules, having managed to throw her off her horse, stood over her with the club in his hand, offering mercy, but that she chose to die rather than surrender the gift from her father.

Upon his return to Mycenae, Hercules gave the girdle to Admete, who was unaware of its meaning and of the blood that had been spent for the sake of her vain request.

THE TENTH LABOR

THE CATTLE OF GERYON

The tenth labor was to be the capture of the immense herds of cattle owned by Geryon, who was a three-bodied and three-headed giant believed to be the strongest creature on earth. He was the son of Chrysaor, whose parents were Poseidon and the Gorgon Medusa, and of Callirhoe, daughter of the Titan Oceanus. Geryon lived on a red island called Erytheia, located in the extreme west, in the stream of Okeanos, the wide river that encircled the whole plain of Earth and where the Sun and stars rose and set; during the night, the Sun sailed over the stream of Okeanos from west to east, using a huge vessel called the Cup of the Sun. Geryon owned herds of beautiful red cattle, which were guarded by the herdsman, Eurytion, and a gigantic two-headed dog named Orthrus.

To reach the extraordinarily remote island, Hercules first crossed the Lybian desert. The heat of the Sun was intense and caused Hercules to suffer so greatly that he threatened to shoot it with his arrows. The Sun begged him not to, and Hercules agreed on the condition that he could use the Cup to cross Okeanos and reach Erytheia. Upon arriving at the channel separating Europe from Africa, Hercules erected as tokens of his journey two pillars facing each other across the straits. They became known as the Pillars of Hercules—that is, the Rock of Gibraltar and the Rock of Ceuta.

As soon as Hercules landed on Erytheia, the dog Orthrus rushed at him, barking menacingly. Hercules quickly silenced the creature with two crushing blows of his famed club—one per head. Eurytion, the herdsman, met a similar end. Hercules then set out to drive away the cattle, but Geryon, alerted by the turmoil, suddenly faced him and challenged him to battle. One of Hercules' deadly arrows pierced one of the monster's foreheads; it split right through the flesh and the bone and stuck at the top of the skull. Red blood darkened the monster's cuirass and legs, and soon one of Geryon's three bodies was leaning toward the floor. Owing to the Hydra's poison, the two other bodies followed suit. Shortly afterward, Hercules loaded the cattle onto the Cup and sailed over Okeanos.

On his way back to Greece, Hercules followed the coasts of Spain, Gaul, Italy, and Sicily, where he became embroiled in numerous battles as well as in numerous romantic affairs. He left his mark everywhere he went, and local cults and sanctuaries honored him even centuries after his passage. It is said by some that the warlike Gauls descended from his union with a tall princess called Galata, who chose him as her lover. As he drove Geryon's cattle through Provence in the plain between Marseilles and the river Rhone, he was attacked by hostile natives. After he had killed many of them with his arrows, his supply ran out. Wounded, exhausted, and unarmed, he knelt down in tears and in desperation appealed to Zeus. The king of the gods, pitying his son, created a cloud from which a shower of stones fell on the plain. With these deadly missiles, Hercules crushed the enemies fleeing in terror. In memory of the episode, the place was called the Stony Plain.

When he passed through the Ligurian Alps he had to fight bands of robbers. He then went down the coast of Italy, traveling through Etruria, and crossed the Tiber with his cattle near the future location of Rome. Hercules slept while some of his finest bulls were stolen by Cacus, a hideous three-headed, fire-breathing shepherd. Cacus lived in a nearby cave littered with the remains of the men and beasts he had devoured, and he dragged the cattle into his cave tail first so that it was impossible to follow their tracks. Eventually Cacus' cache was found, thanks to the bellowing of the stolen bulls. Hercules is said to have smashed each of Cacus' three heads against the cave walls.

At Reggio in Calabria, one of the bulls broke away from the herd and plunged into the sea, where it swam across the strait to Sicily. Some claim that the neighboring country Italy owes its name to this bull, for the natives called it Italus. In Sicily the bull joined the herds of Eryx, who reigned over the Elymi. The king, a son of Poseidon, refused to surrender the animal unless Hercules beat him in a wrestling bout. In the ensuing match Hercules lifted Eryx high into the air, dashed him to the ground, and killed him. Some claim that Eryx had a daughter named Psophis, and that she bore Hercules a son.

Eventually Hercules took the herd across the Ionian Sea, but when they reached the Greek coast, Hera afflicted the cows with gad-flies, which drove them wild. As a result, the herd scattered in the foothills of the mountains of Thrace. Hercules went in pursuit of them but could round up only a few; the rest remained wild and strayed as far as the coasts of the Black Sea and the Scythian desert. During his pursuit of the cattle, Hercules fell asleep one night in the desert. When he woke up in the morning, his chariot horses were missing. He undertook a long and exhausting search, which led him to a wooded area called Hylaea. There he encountered a strange creature, half woman, half serpent, who claimed to have his horses; she added that she would return them only if he became her lover. Not giving him time to answer, the serpent-tail woman embraced him passionately and drew him into her cave, where they spent three intense nights of love. When she finally released Hercules, she asked, "What of the son I now carry in my womb?" Hercules gave her his bow and replied, "If he ever bends this bow, choose him as the ruler of your country!" He then went on his way. She named the child Scythes; he was able to bend the bow and became the ancestor of the Scythian kings. At long last Hercules reached Mycenae with the surviving bulls and gave them to Eurystheus, who eventually sacrificed them to Hera.

THE ELEVENTH LABOR

THE GOLDEN APPLES
OF THE HESPERIDES

When Hera married Zeus, Gaia, the Earth, gave her golden apples as a wedding present. Delighted with the gift, the goddess planted them in her garden near Mount Atlas, in the extreme west, where the chariot horses of the Sun complete their journey every evening. The mountain took its name from the Titan Atlas, who was the guardian of the pillars of Heaven. As punishment for his part in the revolt of the Titans against Zeus, Atlas had to support the sky on his shoulders. Hera, having found out that the daughters of Atlas were stealing from the garden, had the apple tree placed under the protection of Ladon, a dragon with a hundred heads. The dragon never slept, and each of its throats uttered a different sound, so that a cacophony of hisses announced its presence. Three nymphs of the evening, Aegle (brightness), Erythia (scarlet), and Hesperethusa (sunset glow), also guarded the apples; these daughters of Night (Nyx) and Darkness (Erebus) were called the Hesperides, and their names were reminiscent of the sunset sky. Hercules was to bring Eurystheus the golden apples as his eleventh labor.

To find his way to the Hesperides, Hercules was advised to question Nereus the river god, reputed to be omniscient. Nereus was unwilling to help and repeatedly assumed various shapes and appearances, but Hercules tied him up and did not release him until he had revealed the way to the garden.

The son of Zeus first reached the Caucasus, where he found Prometheus chained to the mountain. Prometheus was an immortal Titan who, ages before, had been the champion of mankind against the hostility of the Olympian gods. When Zeus deprived men of fire, Prometheus stole a spark from the forge of Hephaestus and brought it to them. To avenge himself, Zeus had the Titan chained and submitted to an eternal torture by an eagle that devoured his liver every day. Hercules shot the eagle through the heart and freed Prometheus. The Titan not only gave him the directions to Mount Atlas but advised him not to pluck the apples himself.

So when Hercules finally reached the country of the Hyperboreans and found Atlas, who was bearing the whole weight of the sky on his shoulders, he offered to relieve the giant of his burden. In return, Hercules asked that Atlas retrieve three golden apples from the garden. Ever eager for a respite, Atlas accepted on the condition that Hercules first slay the dragon Ladon. The son of Zeus promptly obliged with an arrow shot over the garden wall; the dragon expired in a long, agonized death punctuated by the dwindling sounds of its hundred voices. Hercules then carried the phenomenal weight of the starry sky on his unfailing shoulders while Atlas went to collect three golden apples. Upon his return, the Titan was thrilled by his newfound freedom. He offered to take the apples to Eurystheus himself. Hercules pretended to agree but asked Atlas to support the sky for only a moment more while he put a cushion on his shoulders. The deceiver was easily deceived and resumed his burden. Meanwhile Hercules picked up the apples and went on his way. As for the Hesperides, despairing at the loss of the apples, they turned into trees—elm, poplar, and willow.

On his way back to Mycenae, Hercules traveled through Libya. That country was ruled by Antaeus, son of Poseidon and of Gaia, who used to kill strangers by forcing them to wrestle with him. Antaeus was an accomplished athlete as well as a colossal and ruthless giant who feasted on the flesh of lions and used the skulls of his victims in the construction of a temple designed to honor his father. Challenged to a wrestling match, Hercules removed his lion pelt and rubbed himself with olive oil. When the fight started, he quickly noticed that whenever he tossed Antaeus on the ground, the giant seemed revived and strengthened by his contact with the earth. Thereupon Hercules grabbed him and lifted him high in the air. As he exerted a formidable pressure, the giant's ribs were crushed amid a sinister cracking noise. As a further precaution, Hercules held him aloft until he died.

When Eurystheus received the apples, he was at a loss for what to do with them, so he handed them back to Hercules. In turn, Hercules presented them to Athena, who returned them to the garden, judging that they were the property of the Olympian gods.

THE TWELFTH LABOR

THE CAPTURE OF CERBERUS

The last labor imposed on Hercules was to bring back Cerberus, a monster that had three heads of a dog, the tail of a dragon, and a mane of snakes. Cerberus guarded the entrance of the Underworld. As a preliminary, Hercules had to be initiated into the Mysteries of Eleusis. (It was in that town near Athens that Persephone, who had been abducted by Hades, god of the Underworld, was returned to her mother, Demeter.) The mysteries involved a secret rite in which the initiate was taught how to cross safely to the other world after death.

Guided by Athena and Hermes, Hercules descended into the Underworld from Cape Taenarum at the extreme south of the Peloponnese. His arrival terrified the dead, who all fled, except the Gorgon Medusa and Meleager. At the sight of Medusa, Hercules drew his sword, but Hermes explained to him that she was merely an empty phantom. He aimed an arrow at Meleager, who moved Hercules to tears when he described the tragic circumstances of his own death, caused by his mother, Althaea. When Meleager mentioned that he had a living sister named Deianeira, who was unmarried, Hercules promised to marry her. Near the gates of Hell, Hercules met his friend Theseus; the hero had been put in chains by Hades, thus paying dearly for his invasion of the Underworld in his attempt to carry Persephone away. But Hercules set him free with Persephone's permission. When the son of Zeus came to see Hades and asked him for Cerberus, the god replied, "He is yours if you can master him without using your weapons." Clad only in his lion pelt and indifferent to the furious stings of the barbed tail, Hercules seized the dog's neck and did not relax his crushing pressure until the monster choked and yielded. Hercules then dragged Cerberus and emerged from the Underworld at Troezen in Argolis.

Upon seeing Cerberus, Eurystheus was struck with terror and took refuge in his bronze jar. Eventually Hercules returned the dog to Hades.

This was Hercules' triumphant end to the Twelve Labors, which had started as repentance and humiliation at the hands of his cowardly and unworthy cousin. Unlike the Olympian gods, Hercules did not know that the glory he had won, and the superhuman courage he had shown, would earn him the immortality Zeus had had in mind from the outset.

PART THREE

THE WARRIOR AND THE LOVER: THE CAMPAIGNS OF HERCULES

HERCULES' TROJAN WAR

On his way back from the country of the
Amazons (see the ninth labor), Hercules
landed at Troy. In those days, the city was
incurring the wrath of Poseidon and Apollo,
the two gods who, as punishment for revolt-
ing against Zeus, had been sentenced to serve
a mortal for wages. Laomedon, king of Troy,
had employed the two gods to build the city's
fortifications. But he failed to pay the fee
that had been stipulated when construction
started. Apollo then sent a devastating plague
and Poseidon a sea monster, which preyed
on the inhabitants and ruined the crops.
Laomedon was advised by an oracle to
expose his own daughter Hesione on the
seashore for the monster to devour. Only
then would the curse be removed. Upon

reaching Troy, Hercules found the unfortunate Hesione naked and chained to a rock on the shore. He freed the princess and, being told of the monster, offered to destroy it in return for Laodemon's two immortal white mares, which could run over water. Laodemon had received the mares from Zeus, who, having become infatuated with Ganymede, the king's son, had abducted and carried him off to Olympus. Laodemon accepted Hercules' offer.

Soon the sea monster reached the walls of Troy and opened its gigantic jaws. Instead of battling the creature, Hercules jumped fully armed from the fortifications into its throat and from there made his way to the beast's belly. He then proceeded to destroy it from the inside, butchering the guts and heart with his sword and arrows. The monster died in writhing agony.

Hercules emerged victorious and claimed his reward, but Laomedon once more failed to keep his word. Hercules left Troy enraged and promised to come back and sack the city.

It was only after the completion of the labors that Hercules seized the opportunity to avenge himself. Knowing that the Trojans were formidable adversaries, he recruited an army and organized a fleet of eighteen ships with fifty oarsmen each. They disembarked near Troy, where Hercules and his troops besieged the city. The first assault on the walls was successful, thanks to a daring maneuver by Telamon, who was one of Hercules' most loyal and astute followers. But as he saw Telamon lead the assault in a show of immense bravery, the son of Zeus could not conceal his jealousy and rage. He followed in Telamon's tracks with his drawn sword, but the latter, sensing that the weapon was aimed at him, suddenly knelt down and collected large stones dislodged from the wall. This intrigued Hercules, who asked him what it meant; Telamon replied that he was building an altar to Hercules the Victor. The hero thanked him and continued his assault on the Trojans. He sacked the city and killed Laomedon and all his sons except Podarces, who alone had argued that the divine mares should be awarded to Hercules. Telamon was rewarded with the hand of Hesione, who was allowed to choose one of the prisoners. She chose Podarces, to which Hercules responded by stating that her brother would first have to be sold as a slave and then redeemed. Hesione took off the golden veil that bound her head and gave it as ransom for her brother, who henceforth was named Priam, which means "bought, redeemed." Later in his life, Priam was to become king of Troy, to experience the extremes of good and bad fortune, and to eventually witness the tragic destruction of his city and the deaths of his sons at the hands of the Greeks.

While the fleet was on its way back from Troy, Hera created a powerful storm, which drove the fleet to Cos, an island in the Sporades, off the coast of Asia Minor. All the ships were destroyed except Hercules'. The exhausted and hungry survivors asked a shepherd who was passing by with a flock of sheep to give them a ram; instead, the shepherd, a huge fellow named Antagoras, challenged Hercules to a wrestling match with the ram as the prize for victory. But the islanders rushed to Antagoras' help, thinking he was being attacked. During the ensuing tumult, Hercules and his companions were overcome by their numerous attackers and had to flee. Hercules ended up taking refuge in a hut inhabited by a stout matron, and he put on her clothes to avoid being recognized. The following day, a rested, satiated, and vengeful Hercules, still dressed in the woman's clothes, went on a rampage on the island, and this time he prevailed over his enemies. Some say that after having humiliated the islanders he went on to marry Chalciope, the daughter of the local king, Eurypylus; it is even claimed that he derisively wore female dress during the ceremony, and that since then, Coan bridegrooms wear women's clothes when they welcome their brides home.

Hercules did not stay on the island of Cos for long. Soon after his unusual wedding, Athena guided him to Phlegra, where he was to take part in the battle of the gods against the Giants.

THE BATTLE AGAINST THE GIANTS

The Giants, huge creatures with awful faces and dragon tails, were born of Gaia, the Earth, and Uranus, the sky god. They were conceived from the blood of Uranus, which fell upon the earth when he was castrated by his son Cronos. Gaia stirred them against Zeus because the king of the Olympian gods had sent her elder sons, the Titans, to Tartarus, a part of the Underworld where they were chained; meanwhile Atlas, another Titan, was doomed to carry the sky on his shoulders, and his brother Prometheus had been chained until Hercules released him. Climbing from the Underworld, the Giants rushed to the fields of Phlegra in Thessaly; there, Gaia harangued them, urging them to overthrow the Olympian gods and seize their domains and symbols of power—from Poseidon's sea to Apollo's sun and on to Zeus' thunderbolt. These marching orders were welcomed with enthusiasm, and soon a vociferous and unruly mob of monsters was on its way to the mountains of Thessaly, approaching Mount Olympus. The residence of the gods, usually a place of intrigue and calculation, suddenly became a besieged citadel. The Giants were unmatched in the bulk of their bodies, and their might was invincible. Surpassing all the others were Porphyrion and Alcyoneus, who was immortal as long as his dragonlike tail touched the earth of his origins. The monsters were tearing mountains and piling them one on top of the other to form a ramp from which Olympus could be stormed with boulders and set on fire with burning oaks. An oracle had told that none of the Giants could perish unless a mortal assisted the gods and fought on their side. Gaia was aware of the oracle and was feverishly seeking a medicinal plant to prevent the Giants from being destroyed. But Zeus forbade the Sun and the Moon to shine and thus made it impossible for Gaia to continue the search. The king of the gods culled the plant himself before anyone else could get hold of it. Zeus then sent Athena to the island of Cos to summon Hercules' help. The hero immediately followed the goddess, eager to put his strength and fighting ardor at the service of his father.

Hercules first shot Alcyoneus with an arrow, but the Giant revived upon falling to the ground. Hercules then heeded the advice of Athena and, taking the creature in his arms in an odd embrace, lifted him up in the air until death ensued.

Later in the battle, Porphyrion assaulted Hera. In his frenzied lust for the goddess, he savagely tore her robe and was about to overcome her when Zeus struck him with a thunderbolt and Hercules shot him dead with an arrow. Among the other Giants, Ephialtes was shot by Apollo with an arrow in his right eye and by Hercules in his left eye; Hecate killed Clytius with torches; and Hephaestus mortally wounded Mimas with missiles of hot metal. On the fleeing Enceladus Athena threw an island, which was to become Sicily. One by one the Giants were destroyed by the thunderbolts of Zeus and the arrows of his mortal son.

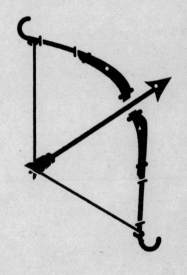

THE MURDER OF IPHITUS

After his labors Hercules returned to Thebes. His marriage with Megara had been unhappy ever since he had slaughtered their three sons, and so he gave her to Iolaus, his nephew and charioteer. As he was looking for a new wife, he heard that Eurytus, king of Oechalia, on the island of Euboea, had offered the hand of his daughter Iole as a prize to any archer who could outdo his four sons and himself. So Hercules went to Oechalia and easily won the contest. Yet the promised bride eluded him, for Eurytus did not keep his word, arguing that Hercules, who had murdered his own children and discarded his wife, was not a desirable bridegroom. Further, Eurytus, who had drunk a great deal of wine after the contest, unjustly accused Hercules of having cheated by using magic arrows. He expressed openly his contempt by calling him a slave of Eurystheus and by expelling him from his palace. Humiliated and stunned, Hercules promised himself that vengeance would be swift and complete.

Unlike his three brothers, Iphitus, the eldest son of Eurytus, disapproved of his father's reneging on his promise and said that Iole should be given to Hercules. And when, shortly afterward, horses were stolen from Euboea, Iphitus refused at first to believe that this was the work of Hercules. The mares and foals had in fact been stolen by Autolycus, a notorious thief, who sold them to the unsuspecting Hercules. As Iphitus, following the tracks of the stolen animals, found out that they led to Tiryns, where Hercules was staying, he grew suspicious of Hercules; but when he met the hero face to face, he stopped short of accusing him and merely asked for his help in the search for the horses. Hercules promised to assist him and offered his hospitality in Tiryns. Yet Hercules had a vague but growing feeling that he was suspected of theft; this, combined with the memory of the disgraceful behavior of Iphitus' father, ignited a concealed but uncontrollable anger at his guest. After a magnificent banquet, Hercules led Iphitus to the top of the highest tower in the city and said to him, "Look around and let me know if you see your mares and foals grazing!" As soon as Iphitus replied that his property was nowhere in sight, Hercules exploded, "You have thus falsely accused me in your heart of being a thief!" And in an attack of murderous rage, he seized the unfortunate Iphitus and hurled him to his death.

Once he awoke from this new fit of madness, Hercules recognized that there was more to the episode than his hot temper: A cowardly murder had taken place, which erased the glory he had earned through his labors. In his need to be purified and to be relieved of the sense of shame that was torturing him, he went to seek the advice of the Oracle at Delphi. The Pythoness gave him a chilling reception: "I have no answer for people who murder their guests!" Hercules responded by sacking the sanctuary and pulling away the tripod on which the priestess was sitting. He added that he would set up his own oracle elsewhere. Apollo suddenly appeared, indignant and eager for expeditious punishment. Zeus had to separate his two sons with a thunderbolt and made them clasp hands in a gesture of friendship. The priestess then made the following pronouncement: "To be purified you must be sold into slavery and serve one master for three years; this is the will of Zeus, who otherwise will never forgive this murder committed in a treacherous manner. The money from the sale is to be given to Eurytus." Hercules submitted and was taken to Asia Minor by Hermes, the god presiding over financial transactions. Offered for sale, Hercules was eventually bought by Omphale, the queen of Lydia. The money was offered to Eurytus, who indignantly refused it and stated that debts in blood are to be repaid in blood.

SLAVERY UNDER OMPHALE

Omphale had been bequeathed the kingdom of Lydia at the death of her husband Tmolus. While hunting on Mount Carmanorium, the king had fallen in love with Arrhippe, a chaste priestess of Artemis. Arrhippe did not respond to his attempts to seduce her and fled to the temple of the goddess. Tmolus ravished her in the sanctuary. The unfortunate Arrhippe hanged herself from a beam after invoking the goddess. Artemis let loose a wild bull, which tossed Tmolus into the air. The king was horribly mutilated by the blow and by his subsequent fall on sharp rocks; he died a few days later.

During his three years of slavery, Hercules faithfully served his mistress. Among other things, he rid the region of the bandits who infested it, with the exception of the two Cercopes. These were a pair of monkeylike dwarves and the cleverest cheats and liars known to mankind. Their mother, Theia, had told them to beware of a certain Melampyges—which means "black buttocks"—but they did not know who this might refer to. One night they tried to steal Hercules' armor, but as they were buzzing around his bed in the guise of blue blowflies, he grabbed them and forced them to assume their real shape. He then slung them upside down from a pole, which he carried across his shoulders. To their consternation, the two Cercopes found themselves staring at Hercules' buttocks; not only were these covered with black hair, a sign of strength, but they had been blackened by the fiery breaths of Cacus during the tenth labor. As the twins suddenly understood their mother's warning, they burst into a fit of laughter. When they explained to Hercules the reason for their merriment, he, too, laughed heartily. And when they started joking about his hairiness, he was so amused that he let them go.

An unusual episode took place at Celaenae,

where lived a farmer named Lityerses. He was a son of Midas, the legendary king of Phrygia who had made the mistake of wishing that all he touched might turn to gold. Lityerses offered hospitality to all newcomers. But then he requested them to compete with him in reaping the harvest, and if they did not surpass him in activity, he would whip them or behead them. After he had heard of the sorry fate of Lityerses' guests, Hercules took part in the challenge, outdid Lityerses, and, without further ado, decapitated him with a sickle. The corpse ended up in the river Maeander.

During the three years of his slavery, Hercules was more a lover than a fighter. When Omphale purchased him, she had in mind her own sensual needs and her wish for offspring as well. Hercules gave her three sons, to say nothing of the numerous children he fathered on her women. The hero's muscular body and his inexhaustible potency were fertile ground for Omphale's unbridled sexual imagination. One day as the two lovers were visiting Tmolus' vineyards, the little god Pan noticed them. This son of Hermes was the god of shepherds and flocks and had an odd appearance, combining the torso of a man and the legs, ears, and horns of a goat. Pan's preference was for remote surroundings such as mountains and caves. He fell in love with Omphale at first sight—and it must be said that she was magnificent in her splendid gown of purple silk embroidered with gold. When Hercules and Omphale arrived in a secluded grotto, they exchanged clothes to amuse themselves. She dressed him in the purple gown and in a tight girdle. After dinner they went to sleep in separate beds, having made a sacrifice to Dionysus, a god who expects marital purity on such occasions. Pan crept into the grotto in the middle of the night and groped his way to the bright cloth of silk. As he feverishly lifted the clothes, Hercules woke up and reflexively kicked him so that the little god crashed across the grotto. Awakened by the din, Omphale promptly understood what had happened, and the two lovers enormously relished the grotesque episode.

Afterward the love affair between the hero and the queen took a slightly different turn.

Hercules was often attired in women's long dresses or petticoats. He wore necklaces, bracelets, and women's turbans. Sitting at Omphale's feet, he learned how to weave. Meanwhile the queen, clad in his lion skin and wielding his club, scolded him or struck him with her slippers when he showed clumsiness in spinning. And she made him tell her all about the Twelve Labors, stories she enjoyed all the more because the unsurpassed hero was her slave.

Thus were the years Hercules spent with Omphale a mixture of glory and humiliation.

PART FOUR

————————

LOVE FOR DEIANEIRA/ HERCULES' DEATH AND APOTHEOSIS

When his enslavement to Omphale ended, Hercules, still without a legitimate wife, thought again of the promise he had made to the ghost of Meleager during his stay in the Underworld (see the twelfth labor). Meleager was the son of Oeneus, king of the Aetolian city of Calydon, and of his wife Althaea. At Meleager's birth, the three Moirai, goddesses of fate, looking like old women spinning, announced that he would live as long as a certain piece of burning wood was not consumed. Althaea carefully preserved the wood. One day, when Meleager was an adolescent, Oeneus failed to perform a sacrifice to Artemis. The irked goddess then sent a huge boar to ravage Calydon. Meleager took part in the hunt along with Atalanta, a virgin huntress with whom he was in love. Atalanta wounded the boar, and Meleager finally killed it and gave her its skin. But subsequently Althaea's brothers tried to take the skin from Atalanta, and Meleager killed them. Hearing of the deaths of her brothers, Althaea allowed the fire to completely burn the piece of wood, and Meleager died at once.

Deeply moved by the young man's tragic fate, Hercules had pledged to marry Deianeira, his sister. Remarkable for her beauty as well as for her passionate and untamed nature, Deianeira had rejected many suitors. It further kindled Hercules' interest to hear that she drove a chariot and practiced the art of war. When the son of Zeus came to Oeneus' palace, he found himself competing with the river god Achelous for the hand of Deianeira. The god was able to assume three shapes: that of a bull, that of a serpent, and that of a man with the forehead of a bull and a beard from which flowed a continuous stream of water. Deianeira did not conceal her repugnance for such a creature and had sworn to die rather than share his couch. But her father was hesitant to turn down the demand of an immortal.

When Hercules openly set out to court Deianeira and soon asked for her hand, Achelous, who assumed his bull-headed human appearance, challenged his rival's claims to divine extraction and added, "If you are really the son of Zeus, then your mother was an adulteress!" The insult marked the beginning of a savage fight in which the bull-headed Achelous promptly met his death at the hands of an enraged and pugnacious Hercules. But Achelous did not waste a second and metamorphosed into a speckled serpent. Hercules' response: "Overall, serpents have not had much luck with me." To avoid strangulation, Achelous resorted to his third embodiment, a charging bull. Hercules then caught the bull by its horns and lifted it high above his head in an incredibly swift motion before hurling it to the ground. One of the horns broke off during the maneuver, which marked the end of Achelous' resistance. And so Hercules won the hand of Deianeira along with her gratitude and admiration.

For some time Hercules lived with Deianeira in Calydon. One day, as he was feasting with his father-in-law, a young lad named Enemus, son of Architeles and a page of Oeneus, splashed Hercules' legs while pouring water on his hands. Hercules impulsively killed him with a blow of his knuckles. All understood that this was an accident; Architeles and Oeneus even granted forgiveness in spite of their sorrow. But driven both by his shame over the senseless killing and by his respect of the traditions, Hercules decided to leave Calydon and went into exile in Trachis with his wife and their young son, Hyllus.

During the journey eastward from Aetolia to Malis, they crossed the flooded river Evenus. The centaur Nessus lived on the bank of the river and ferried passengers across for a fee. It was agreed that Hercules would swim across by himself, while Deianeira was to be carried over. But while ferrying her across and holding her in his arms, Nessus attempted to violate her. Alerted by her screams, Hercules pierced the centaur's breast with an arrow shot from the opposite bank. Near death, Nessus called Deianeira and told her, "If Hercules ever stops loving

114

you and you want to use a love charm on him, mix my seed, which spilled on the ground, with the blood pouring from my wound. With that potion, you should then anoint Hercules' cloth." Profoundly troubled by these words, Deianeira believed him and discreetly collected the ingredients.

Hercules settled in Trachis, but not for long. The proximity of the island of Euboea quickly became an irritant for his restless and ever-vengeful mind. Constantly reminiscing about Eurytus, who had refused to surrender his daughter Iole after the archery contest, Hercules mustered an army to attack Oechalia. The city was stormed and pillaged without mercy, Eurytus and his three sons slain by Hercules himself, their bodies pierced with arrows, and Iole taken captive. When, a few weeks later, the princess was sent to Trachis along with other women from Oechalia, Deianeira was struck by her beauty and her majestic appearance and lamented the tragic consequences that Hercules' passion for Iole had already brought about. Deianeira found the idea of having to endure the presence of a rival under the same roof so intolerable that the love potion suggested by Nessus presented itself as her last hope.

After his crushing victory over Eurytus, Hercules decided to consecrate an altar of thanksgiving to his father, Zeus, at Cenaeum on the island of Euboea. He sent his herald, Lichas, to Trachis to fetch a new cloak for the ceremony. Deianeira smeared a tunic with Nessus' blood and semen and gave it to Lichas. Hercules put it on and proceeded with the sacrifice of a large herd of cattle. As soon as his body warmed the tunic, the poisonous nature of the centaur's fluids became manifest. Hercules uttered a loud and terrifying scream as his skin underwent a dramatic and irreparable corrosion. Beside himself, in excruciating pain, Hercules lifted Lichas by the feet and hurled him into the sea. He then tried to tear the tunic off, but the cloth clung to his body so that he ripped his own flesh to the point of laying bare his bones. As a result of the poison, his blood boiled and burned his entrails. In an attempt to reduce the torture, he plunged into the nearest stream, but to no avail. It is said that these waters have been hot ever since and that this is why the place is still called Thermopylae ("hot passage"). In that sorry state Hercules was taken to Trachis on a ship. During the passage, Hercules, unable to endure the pain, bellowed and gesticulated; around him, his companions wept silently. Though she did not witness Hercules' agony, Deianeira heard of his return and, upon understanding what she had done, hanged herself. Realizing that he was near death, Hercules instructed Hyllus, his son by Deianeira, to marry Iole when he came of age, and announced his intention to die by the fire on the highest peak of Mount Oeta near Trachis. Overcoming the agitation and the weakness caused by the pain that was racking his body, Hercules set out to climb Mount Oeta with the help of his son. He then built a large pyre and climbed onto it after having spread his lion pelt over the platform. When he ordered his terrified companions and servants to kindle it, none obeyed. However, a shepherd named Philoctetes, who was passing by, accepted Hercules' order and set the platform on fire. Out of gratitude, Hercules bestowed his bow and arrows on him. It is said that shortly after the flames

117

started rising, a cloud lifted Hercules to the sky, while thunderbolts fell and disintegrated the pyre. The mortal part of Hercules had been consumed.

For the son of Zeus, a life of immortality among the deities was starting. His father welcomed him and drove him to the Olympian Heaven in his four-horse chariot. Athena, holding his hand, introduced him to his fellow immortals. Hercules was reconciled to Hera, whose resentment had vanished after he had saved her from the Giant Pronomus; and he married her daughter Hebe, the goddess of youth, by whom he had two sons, Alexiares and Anicetus.

It was an apt end to an existence in which every ignominy had been followed by an ascent to unmatched glories. After three such cycles, Hercules had earned the right to a final apotheosis.

AFTERWORD

The legends of Hercules are the most popular and most intricate tales in Greek mythology. Both hero and god, Hercules is a contradictory character who strikingly illustrates the structure, possible origins, and impact of Greek myths. As the reader will have noticed, the main themes of the stories are fights with animals; fights with fabulous creatures, such as Amazons and Giants; heroic deeds, in which Hercules deals with human adversaries; and death metamorphosed into deification.

Structure

Studying Russian fairy tales in the 1920s, Vladimir Propp described a stereotyped sequence of as many as thirty-one elements that can be found in almost every tale, either in its entirety or in part. Some basic functions in a narrative would be as follows: At first, there is a damage, lack, or desire; next, the hero is told to go on a quest; he agrees to do so; he leaves home; he meets someone who puts him to a test; he receives a gift or magical aid; he gets to the place required; he meets an adversary with whom he interacts; he is harmed, but he wins; the initial damage or lack is put right; the hero begins his homeward journey; he is pursued but saved; he comes back without being recognized; there is a wicked impostor, a test, and final success; the hero is recognized; the impostor is punished; the hero marries and becomes king. Every tale contains some combination of these functions. In Greek mythology, the Propp sequence appears in the legend of Perseus and in the labors of Hercules. Thus, to capture the cattle of Geryon (see the tenth labor), Hercules, by command of Eurystheus, sets out on a long journey. He meets Helios, the sun god, from whom he obtains the magical object, the golden cup necessary to cross Okeanos; upon his arrival at Erythreia, the red island, he battles Geryon, the three-bodied master of animals, and seizes the cattle. On the return journey, recurrent adventures with impostors occur, as the cattle get lost or stolen on the way through Gaul, Italy, and Sicily. Hercules' marriage takes place on Olympus after all the labors have been carried out.

Hypothetical Origins

There has been considerable scholarly speculation as to the origins of the legends of Hercules. In *Structure and History in Greek Mythology and Ritual,* Walter Burkert, a Swiss historian of ancient religion, has provided the most elaborate picture of their genealogy. Three directions have been explored: (1) the Near Eastern origins of the legend; (2) the sources of the Geryon myth (the tenth labor); (3) the kinship of the Hercules stories with shamanism, pointing to very ancient links with Paleolithic practices. Burkert sees a basic theme uniting these different threads: Hercules as the embodiment of mastery over animals.

1. The ancient Near Eastern sources: Striking parallels to the myths of Hercules appear at a much earlier date in Mesopotamia from the fourth millennium on: A hero overcomes bulls and lions and beheads a seven-headed snake reminiscent of the Hydra. The hero is named Ninurta, and he is the son of Enlil, the storm god, who corresponds to Zeus, the father of Hercules. On Sumerian seals the hero appears with a lion skin, club, and bow. These similarities persist over time in texts and images ranging from Bronze Age Sumeria to Babylonian epics in which a sea dragon, Tiamat, takes as her allies eleven monsters; all twelve—the number of Hercules' labors—are slain by valiant Marduk. In the Epic of Gilgamesh, the quest for the plant of immortality is comparable to the quest for the apples of the Hesperides. This kind of mythological similarity seems to extend beyond the neighboring Near East and to include Indo-European cultures: In a comparative analysis of warriors in Indian (Indra), Scandinavian (Starkadr), Greek (Hercules), and Iranian (Yima) legends, Georges Dumezil points to a common pattern consisting of three sins, the accumulation of which results in the destruction of the god or hero. In the case of Hercules, the initial refusal to submit to Eurystheus as prescribed by the gods leads to the punishment in the form of madness; then the treacherous murder of Iphitus is punished with enslavement;

122

finally, the betrayal of his wife Deianeira results in the hero's death.

2. *The Geryon tale:* Here we have a theme and variations. Geryon, a three-bodied monster, lives on Erytheia, the red island, far in the west beyond Okeanos, where Sky and Earth meet; his marvelous cattle are watched over by his herdsman, Eurytion, and the two-headed dog Orthrus. To get to the island, Hercules forces Helios, the sun god, to lend him his golden cup, in which the Sun travels every night along the circle of Okeanos from west to east to rise to the sky again. Hercules kills Eurytion, Orthrus, and Geryon, and brings the cattle to Argos. Overall the story fits the Propp pattern previously mentioned. The numerous adventures in which the cattle are lost or stolen during the return trip have given rise to many local traditions, particularly in ancient Italy and Sicily. *Italia* means "land of the cattle," and the Greeks traced the name to the wanderings of Hercules with Geryon's cattle. For the herdsmen of Italy, Hercules was their special protective divinity; the sanctuaries and cults in Italy as well as the narrative itself are probably the reflection of

a pastoral culture: Animals are lost, hidden by mischievous enemies, sought for and retrieved by the strength and cunning of the venerated hero-god. These considerations are far from exhausting the richness of the Geryon tale. The interested reader is referred to Emily Vermeule's *Aspects of Death in Early Greek Art and Poetry* for a clever analysis of the story in the context of archaic Greek culture and its views on death.

3. *The possible connection with shamanism:* In a cattle-raiding myth such as Geryon's, a contrast is apparent between the concreteness of the edible and usable cattle and the need to overcome a mysterious, distant, and monstrous master. Two pieces of evidence link the quest for animals with some mysterious Beyond: shamanism used as hunting magic and cave paintings of the upper Paleolithic. Shamanism is a system of beliefs entailing healing techniques; rites to influence elements (weather) and events (hunting); prophecies; witchcraft; and the ability to converse with spirits. These powers are accessed through trancelike states. In hunting societies, shamanism is intimately bound up with animals

and is used in direct relation to hunting. Such practices have been observed in Eskimo, Siberian, and Amazonian societies. Thus Eskimos of Greenland, who used to live by seal hunting, believed that the seals belonged to a mistress of animals, Sedna, the Old Woman. If a tribe fails to find enough seals, it is due to the wrath of Sedna, who must be appeased by a shaman. In a trance, the shaman sets out to travel to the deep sea, meets Sedna, and asks why she is angry. She says it is because of taboos broken by men and women that she is covered with filth on account of their uncleanliness. The shaman tidies her up, asks for forgiveness, and comes back successful, bringing the animals with him. The hunters start real hunting at once and, filled with optimism, succeed. Multiple geographic variants of similar practices existed or still exist.

The cave paintings of Western Europe, such as Altamira or Lascaux, depict the hunting of wild cattle and wild horses. Does this magnificent art, found in caves difficult to reach, represent a journey to another world where one could meet animals? Some of the paintings have indeed been interpreted as the focus of shamanistic séances. Penetrating the dark caves may have been part of a shamanistic ritual aimed at restoring affluence.

To go back to Hercules, it is conceivable that the legend stems from a Paleolithic pattern in which a deficiency is resolved by a miraculous helper who gets access to the Beyond and brings the wanted animals back. Such a link would provide a different view of Hercules: The hero would not be fundamentally a warrior, but someone whose main function is to tame and bring back animals—cattle, horses, boars, deer, and birds—that are eaten by man. Thanks to him, the mastery of animals that are dangerous, difficult to capture, and cared for by superhuman owners could be transferred to man. In addition to the control of animals, shamanlike themes are present in the Hercules stories, when Hercules goes to the Underworld to overcome Cerberus, when he ascends to Olympus, even when he suffers a fit of murderous madness.

Themes of the Myth: The Complexity and Paradoxes of the Character
The slaying and capture of animals form

126

the prominent motif and, as noted above, may reflect the Near Eastern and possibly Paleolithic sources of the legend.

Struggles with fabulous creatures, Amazons, Centaurs, and Giants, are another central element of the myth. In contrast, the heroic deeds of Hercules as a warrior—e.g., the sacking of Troy—play a relatively minor role. The dramatic death of Hercules stands out in Greek mythology. His jealous wife Deianeira (whose name means "man-destroying") sends him a poisoned garment that causes such horrible burns that he immolates himself on a pyre of wood. Hercules then ascends through the flames to the gods. Among the earliest literary texts, the apotheosis is mentioned in the *Odyssey*; however, in the *Iliad*, Hercules is made to die.

At first sight, Hercules, with his unmatched strength, recurrent victories, and inexhaustible sexual potency, is an unequivocal hero. It turns out, however, that the hero can behave like a slave, a woman, or a madman; and the end of his mortal life is horrific. A son of Zeus, Hercules is a subject of Eurystheus, the king of Mycenae, who obeys Hera. Hercules' very name means "Hera's glory" (*kleos*), yet he is the victim of unrelenting persecution by Zeus' jealous wife. Hercules' enslavement by Omphale, the Lydian queen, is presented as atonement for his having murdered Iphitus in a noticeably treacherous manner; while Hercules spins the thread, Omphale dresses in his lion pelt and brandishes the ax. Ultimately, the fit of madness during which he slays his wife and children in Thebes illustrates to the extreme the paradoxical nature of a myth in which the hero vacillates between omnipotence and humiliation.

The madness and death of Hercules have served as material for two tragedies: Euripides' *Heracles* and Sophocles' *The Women of Trachis*. In *Heracles*, Euripides modifies the chronology of the episode of madness to take place after the twelfth labor; while Hercules goes down to the Underworld, Lycus seizes power in Thebes after having killed King Creon, father of Hercules' wife Megara. He threatens Megara with death, along with her three young sons by Hercules, and Amphitryon. Upon returning, Hercules saves his family and kills Lycus. But Hera sends gorgon-faced Madness, who drives the hero to kill his own children, thinking they are Eurystheus' children, and Megara.

Grieving and despairing as he recovers from his madness, Hercules is comforted by Theseus, the king of Athens, whom he has brought back from the Underworld and who takes him away to Athens to be purified.

In *The Women of Trachis,* Sophocles describes the torments Deianeira experiences in questioning her husband's love and the agony and death of Hercules, which resulted when Deianeira used a love potion provided by Nessus, the centaur. The contrast between the private anguish of Deianeira and the brutal crescendo of Hercules' sufferings is all the more striking as the two characters do not meet in the play.

The Impact of the Myth on Greek and Roman Society

The cults of Hercules were widespread in the Greek world, expressed through sanctuaries and festivals (particularly meat banquets). A popular cult figure, Hercules was portrayed as an omnipresent helper and averter of evil (*alexikakos*). He was invoked on every occasion of surprise or anguish in the form of exclamations: *Herakleis!* for the Greeks, *Mehercule!* for the Romans.

Beyond his popular appeal as a good-humored, muscular beef eater and as a hero, Hercules was considered the prototype of the ruler propelled by divine endorsement. As such, he was an inspiration for ambitious potentates from Alexander the Great to Roman emperors. In addition, the myth blurred the boundary between the human and divine, making the company of gods accessible to inspired mortals.

On the other hand, for the philosophers of the Hellenistic times and their Roman followers, Herculean mythology was of little relevance to their work of analysis and their treatment of human passions and emotions. Thus, in Book V of his *De Rerum Natura* (*On Nature*), written in the first century B.C., Lucretius minimizes the hero's domination over the monsters of the external world, contrasting it with the praise of Epicurus, whose philosophy is said to have tamed the monsters of the inner world—i.e., the soul's passions and desires (fear, arrogance, debauchery, longing for luxury, and idleness).

Conclusion

There is more to Hercules than meets the eye. Far from being a Rambo of the ancient world, our hero is sufficiently rich to lend himself in turn to epic, tragic, or comic representations. Hercules seems to be a link between Greek culture and more ancient cultures from the neighboring Near East. Even more importantly, the patterns discernible in the legends pertaining to the hero may point to connections with the Indo-European sphere as well. Finally, the ever-recurring motif of the capture and control of animals indicates that Hercules may be a vestige of magical and religious practices dating back to the prehistory of mankind. This should not prevent us from admiring what is specifically Greek in these stories: the beautiful complexity of some of the narratives, and the peculiar relationship between men and gods, with their unmistakably Greek way of highlighting the divine in man and the human in the gods.

Bibliography

Walter Burkert. *Creation of the Sacred—Tracks of Biology in Early Religions.* Cambridge: Harvard University Press, 1996.

———. *Greek Religion.* Cambridge: Harvard University Press, 1985.

———. "Heracles and the Master of Animals." In Burkert, *Structure and History in Greek Mythology and Ritual.* Berkeley: University of California Press, 1979.

Georges Dumezil. *L'idéologie tripartie des Indo-Européens.* Bruxelles: Editions Latomus, 1958.

Martha Nussbaum. *The Therapy of Desire.* Princeton: Princeton University Press, 1994.

Emily Vermeule. *Aspects of Death in Early Greek Art and Poetry.* Berkeley: University of California Press, 1979.